RIDER'S TALES

RIDER H. CLEMONS

Superior Publishing LLC.

RIDER'S TALES

CONTENTS

Superior Publishing LLC, 2023
662-295-9893

I would like to dedicate this book to
two of the greatest people I have known...
Laila Nedra Clemons
Kenneth O'Brian &
Chip Pruett

CHAPTER 1

A Path to Wealth and Riches

The year was 1975, in West Point Mississippi, and I never had friends like the ones I had when I was thirteen.

"Anyone else fed up with the Democrats making Nixon resign from office? He had nothing to do with Watergate! And the Democrats still did him wrong." I said.

Then there was an Irish immigrant Cole O'Connor.

" Knock off them American politics and concentrate on the card game so I can win ." Said Cole.

And then there was Jake Jackson He was the leader of our group

"Beat those card ladies ha ha ha" laughed Jake.

"Hey, you guys wassup with it." Said Ben Brown as he walked into the clubhouse.

"Ben, please. We're busy playing go fish."

"This is way better than go fish..." said Ben

"....Do you guys want to find George Washington's treasure."

"Ben, it's 1975...." I said.

"Please re-enter the clubhouse in a more stereo-typically southern, preaching man cartoon style."

"Lord almighty! I done find me a map to Washington's treasure down in the woods

Sho' 'nough, I thought I'd go crazy when I saw me that map" said Ben

"Ben calm down. You're not making any sense man." I said.

So we packed our stuff the next day and went out on an adventure where anything is possible. When we set out that day first thing, We decided to cut through Old Man River's junkyard, even though legend had it that any child caught climbing the fence ran the risk of being attacked by the old man's demon dog who storms the junkyard.

"I've got a bad feeling about this y'all." Said Ben

"Hey! What in the Sam Hill are you kids doing here?" Yelled Old Man River.

"Oh, shoot It's him! Said Jake.

"That's right. I'm Old Man River. I own the junkyard. I'm only mad because all my stuff is nothing but garbage. Why can't I have nice stuff?"said Old Man River.

"Loki, sic them. Sic them, boy!"

"Ah Run boys run for your lives." I said as we ran away from Loki the demon dog.

But Now however , he did say, "Sic them, boy!"

But what I heard was, '"Loki, go to the White House and talk to President Ford about sliding down the airplane stairs

"Glad America didn't know what I did" said President Ford.

"I think America has known to much" said Loki the demon dog

As we got away and lost Loki we started to walk down to Cedar Bluff, which is a long journey, so we stopped at the train tracks.

"Dang man, this trip is really dangerous shouldn't we at least have taken a drive or something?" Asked Cole.

"You do know we are thirteen? We don't have cars until we are at least 18." I said.

"Wait Guys? Anyone know when the next train is scheduled by any chance?" Asked Jake.

"Don't worry. If a train comes, I'll warn you in at least slow motion. But I think the train tracks should be banded." I said.

As three of the guys walked away, for a moment I ended up standing there feeling the vibration of the train coming so I warned the others.

" Freight Train!" I yelled in slow motion

As we all screamed and ran away from the train, Jake slipped on the train tracks and got his legs, ran over by the train.

"Ow My legs! What a horrible pain!"

After that, we camped at night and Cole Ben made Jake a wheelchair out of a car seat and two bike wheels that they got from Old Man River's junkyard

"Hey, sorry you got paralyzed, Jake." I said.

"That's all right. I'm still living." Said Jake.

"But Thanks again for going all the way back to the junk-yard to get this wheelchair y'all made me

"Boy, was Old Man River ticked off." Said Cole

The next morning, we looked at the map and found Washington's Treasure so we started digging. We opened the treasure chest, and found diamonds and gold.

"Well, here it is, we are rich now." We said
And singing the Jefferson's theme song and dancing having a good time celebrating

"Out of my way, you little rebels scum I'm taking credit for finding this treasure" said Rogue Roland for he was the meanest guy in town, and his whole clan Abraham Andrew, Carter Calvin & Bill Buchanan

"Hey y'all! What, are we beating kids up or something?" Said Bill Buchanan.

"Now you kids go off! We'll take it from here." Said Carter Calvin.

"Kiss my grits, you file demon ." I said as I was having the right to bear arms.

"This ain't over, Clemons...." said Abraham
"I mean, you have a gun in your hands right now.
But tomorrow, I'll say you shot me and let the law put you in jail for no reason!"

"Oh. Yeah, I guess you could do that, huh?" I said.
"I mean, we do live in the same town. And I don't have any proof, to defend myself with since I'm the one with the gun
Boy, I can't be in jail I'm too young for that ok take it!"

We never forgot that wonderful summer. And eventually we all went our separate ways. Jake learned to live without the use of his legs and even went on to play in the Special Olympics, and became the first Mississippian to win the Special Olympics. Ben grew up and went on to become the first black mayor of West Point Mississippi Actually, I'm not even joking about that. West Point does have the first black mayor in the year 2021. Can you believe that? I swear to God. Look it up on the internet. He's an amazing guy. Ethan grew up to become the owner of a West Point's famous bar called, Sopranos. And I became a great Arthur wrote many books, and became very famous in the United States. All four of us lived happily ever after.

THE END!

CHAPTER 2

From Prison to Repent

It was 1956, the first time I laid eyes on
Patrick O'Brian,I didn't think much of him.
He was an Irish drink of beer. The kind of
beer that you know your friend got, the
cheap kind and not from the good kind.
"Six packs of cigarettes says the Irish one
breaks first tonight." I Nicholas Clemons,
said.
"You're on. I'll take the Elvis wannabe looking one." Said inmate number 0347

**Meanwhile a month later at the court
yard....**

A month went by before Patrick said few
words to someone. As it turned out, that few
words was me.
"Cure for polio." Said Patrick
Later on, Patrick came back to me with more
than just a few words.
"I understand you're a man who knows
how to get stuff in here."

"I've been known to smuggle in stuff." I said.

"Well I need stuff. Can you get it for me?" Said Patrick

"What do you need from me?" I said.

"Well what I need is nothing more then a rock hammer to carve us Presidents out of stone but also not trying to get out of here." Said Patrick

"Wow that's impressive do you think that you can be able to carve me a statue of First Ladies out of stone?"

"Sure man whatever…" Said Patrick "…. You know something we've only had one conversation, but I can tell we're gonna be lifelong friends."

The next day

"Inspection!" Said the Chief of Rankin During the inspection, the warden looks for Patrick O'Brian to cut him a deal but one thing everyone should know never make a deal with the devil himself.

"Are You Patrick O'Brian?" asked the warden

"I don't know. Are you?" Laughed Patrick "I'm just joking with you, What can I do for you?"

"I do understand that you make President figurines." Asked the Warden.

"Oh, Andrew Jackson, awesome!

"   Well, anyway, I'm a pretty corrupt liberal blue guy, so I figured I could buy your figurines and keep the money as well do we have a deal?"

" I don't know. I'm not sure" said Patrick

"Oh Come on now. I'll even crippled that guy who fights you in the shower." Said the warden.

" Ain't nobody trying to fight me any-where ." Said Patrick.

"Too late for that." Said the warden, as the guard started to beat on an inmate Peter Kendrick, and broke both of his legs.
Two things never happened again after that. Peter Kendrick, never ever walked again any-more, and Patrick's burps never made a smell ever again.

Meanwhile on the first day of spring
Thanks to the US president figurines Patrick carved, he landed a non-paying job repaint-ing the warden's office this Spring.

"Okay, you repaint the warden's office while I go take a quick break." said chief. While Patrick repaints the wardens office. He finds a record of a band called Kiss in the wardens desk & plays it on the intercom.
"You gotta lose your life in Detroit Rock City
Twelve o'clock, I gotta rock!
There's a truck ahead, lights staring at my eyes
Oh my God, no time to turn"
To this day, I have no idea what those folks was singing about.
Like, literally no idea.
I don't know where the Detroit Rock City is but I assume that it's a city full of death in every corner darkness In every street to cover up the fact that it's A horrible way to die more ways then Mondays

"Patrick, I think you know why I've called you in here today for.
A prison is an environment which requires the highest level of discipline and that scheme you pulled today made a lot of people look very stupid," said the warden

"Look, Mr.Warden, we got it rough in hell. I just thought we could use a little music is all."

"Music is expressly forbidden inside Rankin prison doors & walls."

"My oh Gosh ! How can you be such a devil?" Asked Patrick

"I'm sorry. What did you just call me?" Asked the warden

"The devil it means that You're being a mean person ." Said Patrick

"Three months in the hole…." Yelled the warden " …. Or am I being mean now?"

"No, now you're just being a sick man " said Patrick.
That time in the dark hole changed old man Patrick

"I'm getting out of here tonight, Nicholas. I'm gonna take the sewer pipes to the skunk swamp." Said Patrick

"Wow man Where are you going once you get out?" I asked

"West Point, Mississippi." Said Patrick

"Sounds tremendously fantastic!" I said.

"Well, actually, it's a small town but a huge heart for Green-Wave pride! Hey listen Nicolas when you get a chance to get out of here, I want you to do something for me.Up out in the country of Cedar Bluff under the only bridge there's a stone that has no business being there.Under that stone is a box with something I want you to have. Of course, now I think about it, I've been in here 16 years and all these landmarks are based on possibly outdated observations. That whole area could be a Burger Prince by now. If it is, pick yourself up some nice cheap burgers and good luck of life to you." Said Patrick

Two days later....

"Inspection." Said the Chief.

As all the prisoners walked out of their cells I looked in Patrick's cell he has not walked out of his cell yet or did he?

"O'Brian, O'Brian? O'Brian, you better get your Irish butt out here before you make me beat your....." said the Chief as he stopped and realize that Patrick was gone.

Meanwhile during the search for Patrick

"Where is he? Where is O'Brian?" asked the warden

"I don't know, sir. For he is nowhere to be found." Said chief.

"I want him found right now! Not after lunch not after your t.v. shows, but right now!

God, I'm so angry I could just throw a knife at that poster of JFK, said the Warden as he threw his knife at the poster of JFK, then realizes there's a giant hole behind JFK's poster.

What the warden and his boys didn't realize

was that Patrick O'Brian had escaped from
Rankin county Prison two nights before.
Patrick crawled to freedom through
600-yards of horrible I don't wanna think
about it!
Patrick O'Brian, the only Irish man who
crawled through a river of sewer and came
out clean on the other side of the free world.
The next day, I saw my probation officer,
hoping I get out of prison at least on probation
"Do you believe in your best judgment that
you have been rehabilitated?" Said my probation officer
"Rehabilitated?..." said I
"It's just a stupid made-up liberal word so
blue boys like you can sit behind a desk,
wear a blue donkey fancy suit, and feel most
important.
You're a jerk for that."
So my probation officer noticed that I had
courage to stand up for myself, so he got me
out a Rankin county
When I got out of Rankin county
There was only one thing on my mind.
The one promise I made to a good friend that
I had to keep so I went to Cedar Bluff to the
only bridge there is and found the stone and
saw the box under it so I open the box read a
letter written by Patrick along with $45,0000
"Dear Nicolas if you've come this far, thought
I'd say congratulations on your freedom. You
remember that green town in Mississippi
right?" Said Patrick

" Yes I do" said I as i looked up from the letter
I met up with Patrick O'Brian in West Point, Mississippi we became friends forever... became brothers & happily ever after.
The End!

CHAPTER 3

The Private Noir

I thought I'd seen it all. But that's the thing about city of West Point You never know what's hiding under the hard shell of a crab.The Great Depression hit the city hard. FDR announced we had nothing to fear but fear itself.
The depression smashed America to bits, covered in broken dreams during the depression in the United States
The country nothing more than a sad and colorless place
Which of course meant drinking was very cool, and everyone did it all the time A lot of it. It was horrible. The name's Otis, Otis Clemons. And I'm a private eye.
My office was in the Pecos building. All the businessmen there had ideas of their own
"Well, Otis , what did you find out?" Said Martin White
"Now hold on..." said Otis

"…it's 8:00 a.m. Let me go ahead & fix you a drink right quick. So, I tailed your wife. Sorry, man she's having an affair with a natural enemy"

"Ah, too bad. I guess she's always the maple, but I'll always be nothing more than the sap." Said Martin

"There you go. You're gonna be okay. But if you need anything else, let me know." Said Otis

"Thanks, Otis.I owe you one big time," said martin

"Mr. Clemons?" Said my assistant named Ms. Jenny Apple-bottom

"Yes Ms. Apple-bottom." Said Otis

"there's a beautiful woman here to see you." Said mrs.Apple-bottom."

"May I come in, detective Clemons." Said a beautiful woman named Hazel Pruett I'll never forget the day she walked in my office one of those women that drive you insane with her beauty.

"What brings you here?" Asked Otis

"So, Mr.Clemons , I'm here because my sister has been kidnapped by the Irish mafia her name is Frances Pruett." Cried hazel

" oh, come on now quit the waterworks already,When did you last seen her with the mafia?" Asked Otis

"She was talking to the Irish godfather, known as Mr. E " said hazel

"Mr.E you say!" Said Otis

" She was working at his strip club called the pony bar & grill " Said hazel

Meanwhile at the pony…..
As Otis watches the women dancing
The dane walked up to him to talk to him
"You wanted to see me good looking." Said the Dane.
"I'm looking for Francis.have you seen her by any chance." Said Otis
" Francis!" Said the Dane as she spits her name "I don't remember and don't care."
" or maybe they should be able to help you remember right?" Said Otis as he offers money to the dane
"Maybe your getting warmer." Said the Dane
Then Otis offers diamonds, and gold to the Dane
"Ok now I remember I saw her a couple of nights ago with Mr.E"
" Where they go do you remember?" Said Otis
"I don't know I do not care" said the Dane
"Hey is this guy bothering you…." Said the Irish gangster "…. Because he's bothering us."
So the Irish gangsters that works for Mr.E threw him out of the the bar into the dark alley
" Keep your American nose out of our business. Do you wanna know what happens to an American that comes in Irishman's business? Said the other Irish gangster with a knife
"I don't know free scotch on the rocks." Said Otis as he was being sarcastic.

"Oh no they get hurt really bad." Said the Irish gangster as he cut otis tie in half.
" And next time is the neck! understand? " Said the Irish gangster.
I was down on one luck, but I was still Kicking just fine so I went to see an old friend from the police force they call him the chef
"Hey Otis what's bring you here?" Said chef
"I'm looking for Mr. E do you know where they hangout at?" Asked Otis
"I heard they are always hanging out at the dock downtown why they hangout there I will never know." Said chef
"Thanks chef!" Said Otis
Meanwhile at the dock downtown West Point And sees Frances tied and taped up by Mr. E and the his Irish gangsters so Otis goes stealthily hid in the shadows like a ninja then all of a sudden lights come on then the other gangsters ends up catching him and puts a gun to his head
"Mr. E !" Said Otis "wait until I tell the D.A.
"O please you ain't telling no one anything ." Said Mr. E
"...And besides have you meet my secret partner in crime"
Then all of a sudden hazel walks out of the shadows of the docks
"Im sorry detective for betraying America it's the only way to save my sister." Cried hazel
"Well I knew you were always crooked. I just didn't want to see it." Said Otis
"Any last words American." Asked Mr. E

"Just a few…. chief, Martin I found them."
Yelled Otis as he whistled for back up
" well looks Like the law, finally caught up to
you Mr.E ." Said chief
"We got right we're we want you." Said
martin
"Oh no it's the cops." Said Mr.E
"Run away every Irishman for himself!"
They shoot at Mr. E and his gang & Irish
gangsters trip over the table and fall & get
hurt
The job is done Francis is saved. The law
finally arrested hazel, Mr. E and his Irish
mafia gang. The Irish mafia gang empire has
finally fall.
Otis walks into the fog and lived happily ever
after the end

CHAPTER 4

That 40's Show

In the year of 1945, in the Southern town of West Point Mississippi, there was this family, the Columbus's. The breadwinner of the house, Bobby Columbus and his lovely wife Cindy and together they had four sons Lake the first born son, Ryder the great one, Hank the handful & Hannah the only daughter. This is their story after World War 2.
It all started that day that Bobby and his three sons were playing catch on their front yard while Cindy and Hannah fixed supper.
"Hey Dad! Asked Ryder, I overheard the folks talking. Can I ask you a question about women?"
"Of course, son. Y'all are a young men now. It's natural to be so curious." Said Bobby.
"Thanks dad, so what's a ducky-style ?" Asked Hank.
"Never mind what the folks have said. If you want to have fun with your girl, try slow

dancing. It's fun, romantic and good for your physical and emotional health."
"Cool that sounds about right." Said Lake.
Few minutes later, supper was called. Everyone was gathered at the dinner table and the family ate while they listened to the radio.
" This is WCBI on radio 6. Our top story this evening, Frank Sinatra will be appearing tupelo, Mississippi's BancorpSouth Arena this Sunday night."

"Wow, Frank Sinatra! O my gosh, Can we get a television set please?" Asked Cindy.

"Sorry, Honey…" said Bobby. " We don't have the money for it."

"Why don't you just buy a TV for the weekend, watch Frank Sinatra and then return it on Monday morning and say it doesn't work?" Said Lake.

"Man Lake, even after the war you're still a crook." Said Hannah.

"That's a good idea son." Said Bobby.

"Hang on sweetheart, why don't I get a job and help pay for it." Said Cindy.

"No wife of mine is gonna have a job." Yelled Bobby. "Who's gonna do all the cleaning and the cooking?" Hannah would do it, but she's not old enough to do everything by herself, a woman's place is in the kitchen!"
The next night, Columbus invited the Ravens over for supper to watch Frank Sinatra on their very first brand new TV.

"Well, we got some time before Frank Sinatra comes on." Said Mr Raven

"Yeah, how did y'all get a new TV anyway

they must cost a fortune?" Asked Mrs. Raven.

" I don't know I was walking around the house after a long day of hard work and I found more money in the swear jar." Said Bobby.

"Good evening. This is WCBI, previously on Radio 6 News. Tonight, We bring you a special report. Women in the workplace is it a blessing or is it a national disgrace?" While they're watching the news about women in the workplace, Bobby sees Cindy on TV of her secretly working in a factory.

"Cindy, is that you on TV? You secretly went behind my back and took a job when I told you not to?" Asked Bobby.

"I did,I'm sorry I just had to take a job so that way we can afford the TV. That's why the swear jar was full of money. Also, I was tired and sick of always staying at the house all the time and never being able to leave the property of the house." Said Cindy, whom is also fighting for female rights and independence.

"Well, all I know is you're gonna quit your job." Said Bobby.

"No I'm not you can't make me." Said Cindy

"Quiet, Frank Sinatra is now on." Said Lake

"Ladies and gentlemen, Mr. Frank Sinatra." Said WCBI news reporter.
As they all first looked at Frank Sinatra, the Raven's found out that hes an Italian.

"What Frank Sinatra's Italian Sweetheart? Did you know about this?" Asked Mrs. Raven.

"Come on Love let's go down the street for some frog legs for tonight's gonna be jumping like crazy." Said Mr Raven.

The next day....
Bobby's sitting on the couch watching TV Cindy walks in from work.

"Bobby I thought you were taking the TV back." Said Cindy

"Well Cindy, I've been thinking..." Said Bobby.
"....You can keep your job so we can afford the TV."

"That's great news honey I'd like that very much." Said Cindy

The next week...
So Bobby sat on the couch watching TV going through the channels and saw the television commercial about fried chicken with 11 herbs, and spices and all of a sudden, Bobby got hungry. He was in the mood for fried chicken but then Cindy walks in feeling tired and restless after having a hard weeks work.

"Honey I'm home...." said Cindy.

"...I don't know how you do it Bobby."

"Did you bring any chicken home or do we have any chicken?" asked Bobby.

"Just working day & night & I'm exhausted, and I miss my family so much." Cried Cindy

"The chicken, I'm talking about has

eleven herbs and spices, they say its tremendously delicious and very crunchy."

"Well anyways I gave my notice, and tomorrow's my last day. So I guess we have to get rid of the TV after all." Cried Cindy

The next month....

"Bobby I got a surprise for you." Yelled Cindy as Bobby comes inside after work and opens the gift.

"A television set...." Said Bobby. "We can't afford that. I thought you quit your job?"

"This is what we were making all along. The only reason I wanted to work was to make this for you because I love you." Said Cindy.

"Oh, Cindy you're the greatest wife of all times. The best wife that any man could ever have." Said Bobby as he kisses Cindy then slow dances with her

The End

CHAPTER 5

Tribute to My Grandmother

Nedra Clemons
was my grandmother. She was born on
September 24, 1946. Her favorite president
was former president, John F. Kennedy. She
was very well-known in West Point through
politics. She used to campaign for former

Mayor, Robbie Robinson. Through her years in life, she was a very jolly woman. She cares about a lot of people, especially her family, whom she loved most. She has always loved her two sons that she raised as a single mother James Richard and William "Billy" Allen Clemons and her five grandchildren she loved a lot River Allen, Rider Hunter, Dylan, Harley Jerry Wayne, and Montana Rain Nedra graduated from West Point high school in the year of 1966 with a 100% full blooded diploma. When I had nowhere else to go, she took me in in her home with open arms and raised me like I was one of her own children even times when I didn't deserve it, she was always a forgiving person to lot of people for the wrongs and sins they've done. She told me to never ever give up, even when I win or lose, never give up to always keep fighting for what's right. I remember me and her did a 2016 bet where she voted for Hillary Clinton and I voted for Donald Trump she told me that if her president won I would massage her feet everyday for four years. And I told her that if my President won she hast to pay me $45 every month for four years but when Donald Trump won the election in 2016, I told her not to pay me and never make a deal with the Lord.

CHAPTER 6

Tribute to My Dear Friend

Kenneth O'Brian

Mr. Kenneth O'Brian was a veteran who served his country not only that, but he worked all of his life and became one of the wealthiest men in West Point Mississippi Irish but Wealthy. I remember when I first met him, I went to see his grandson, and Mr. O'Brian came in the room. He looked upset, and I was very scared of him at first because he look like he was going to snap the closest hand but when me and him started talking I could see that he was a very nice man. He was a great man. He was loved by billions of people in West Point. He was love most by his family. He wasn't like everybody in Old Waverley, which everybody in Old Waverley was snotty. He was like the Waltons rich he was country, enjoyed life of nature, always going fishing, hunting and loving his family every day whom he loved most of all. He loved his beautiful wife, Mrs. Pat O'Brian, who is a great strong woman, their children and all of their grandchildren. I will always miss our talks on the phone when I used to call him once a week to check on him. Ever since I first met him I always wanted to be his friend. I will always enjoy our conversations our chats, and our talks.

Tribute to My Father

Chip Pruett was a born in the year of May 10, 1967 and later passed away on August 10, 2018. Chip Pruett had a troubled life, but turned his life to the Lord Jesus Christ, and became a very successful businessman like his father, Clovis Pruett Jr. Chip Pruett, liked to go out of town and work, not for him, but for his family whom he loved more than anything. Through his life, he has always love my mother Candy and became a father-figure to me, when my father was absent. At the time, Chip Pruett, always gave me the most greatest advice anyone could ever have as a child. He was there for me when I had no one else. I remember when I was little, I had cried real hard and he came to me and wiped my tears away. He was a caring man who loved his children and me. He loved his grand kids.

I miss him more than anyone and I love him so much. Now he is building mansions and castles in heaven.

My name is Rider Hunter Clemons I was born in West Point Mississippi on April 27, 1998. I have the same birthday as former US 18th President Ulysses S. Grant & Coretta Scott King who is The wife of the civil rights leader named Dr. Martin Luther King jr. and of course, uncle Si Robertson from duck dynasty. My grandparents are Lalia Nedra Clemons who wants the 1st to campaign for former mayor Robbie Robertson, my grandfather is named Robert Lee Ryals & my parents are Ms Candy Herron & William Clemons aka Billy Clemons my siblings are River Allen Harley Jerry-Wayne & my half baby sister Montana Rain.

Rider has a full kind heart of patriotism who puts God family & America first his dream is to be successful & to open his own business he may have autism but he never let that stop him from reaching his Goals Rider graduated at West Point high school in the year of 2017

www.ingramcontent.com/pod-product-compliance
Lightning Source LLC
Chambersburg PA
CBHW040801010826
48981CB00028B/8